Peachtree

†HE
WI*TCH
BOY

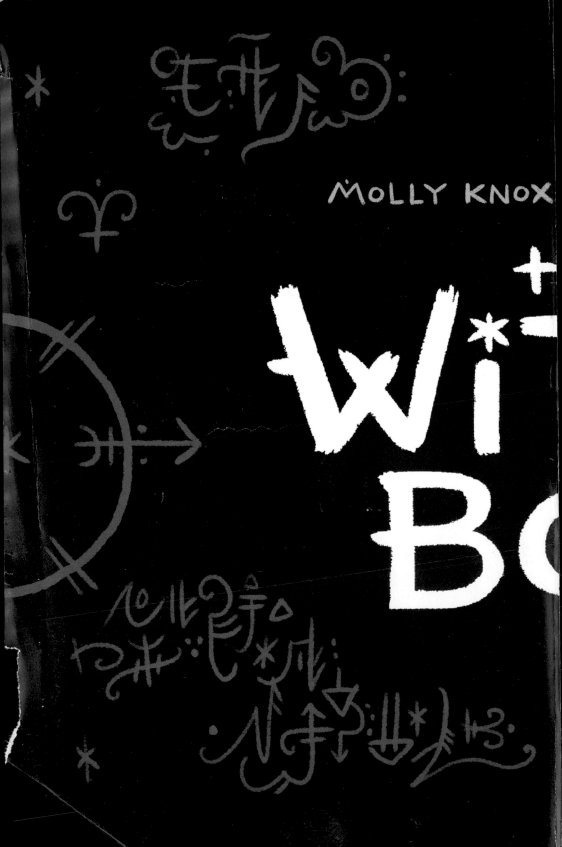

OSTERTAG

HE
TCH
OY

AN IMPRINT OF
SCHOLASTIC

Grandmother

Kieran

Jessamine

Holly

Tohor

Hazel

Linden

Brome

Persimmon

Juniper

Aster

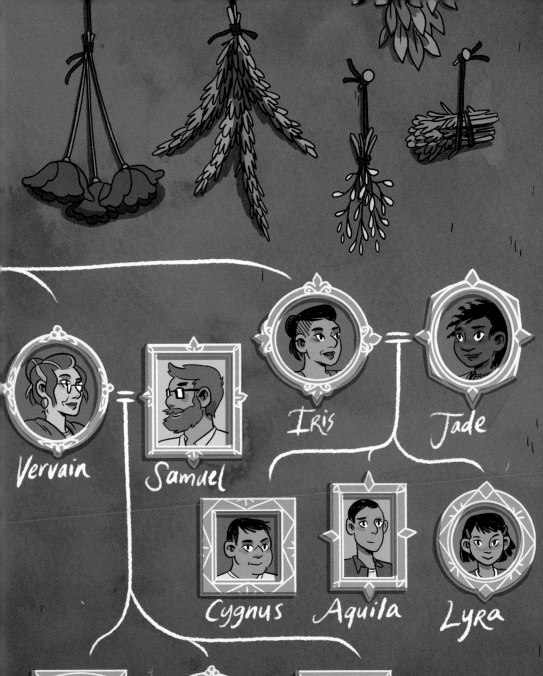

Vervain

Samuel

Iris

Jade

Cygnus

Aquila

Lyra

Sedge

Ivy

Tupelo

This book is dedicated to Wayfinder, the summer camp in upstate New York where I first learned about magic.

Library of Congress Control Number Available

ISBN 978-1-338-08952-3 (hardcover)
ISBN 978-1-338-08951-6 (paperback)

10 9 8 7 6 5 4 3 2 1   17 18 19 20 21

Printed in China   38
First edition, November 2017
Edited by Amanda Maciel
Lettering and color by Molly Knox Ostertag
Additional color by Niki Smith, Barbara Geoghegan, and Shannon Murphy
Book design by Molly Knox Ostertag and Phil Falco
Creative Director: David Saylor

Aster!

SWING

HA HA HA HA HA

This lesson isn't for you -- these girls are learning secrets!

But I want to --

Off with you!

Aster, child, what's wrong?

But, Aster, that magic isn't for you.

How many times do I have to explain that?

But I want to learn it!

Women and men have different types of magic, and witches pass down their knowledge from mother to daughter. That's how it is and how it's always been, my son.

But it's not like there's nothing for you! Soon your shapeshifting will begin, and with it, the ability to see demons and to fight them.

You'll be one of the men.

. . . Don't want to shapeshift . . .

sigh

Did you know that Grandmother is a twin?

She had a twin brother.

Mikasi.

Now, Grandmother is very steady and wise, and always has been, but her brother had no patience or wisdom.

He wanted what he couldn't have: his sister's magic.

11

Why'd Sedge have to go and get Aster? He's never good in this . . .

Okay, so this time let's split up and come at the hill from two angles.

Aquila will probably be their lookout, and he can already shift, so we've got to watch out because he'll probably be a bird --

Why are you in charge, Sedge? Why not let someone who can shift handle the strategy?

Because I'm so charming, obviously!

And I like doing strategies.

Aren't you supposed to tell me not to be doing this?

If you're going to be playing with witchery, at least get it right.

Which one are you, again?

Aster, Grandmother.

Well, just be careful, m'boy.

I wasn't doing anything!

Can I have some?

I'm Charlotte. Charlie.

Can you, um . . . not tell anyone you saw that? With the berries?

What did you even do?

You don't go to Sterling Junior High, do you? I'd have recognized you.

No, I, uh . . .

No, I go to a . . . different . . . school.

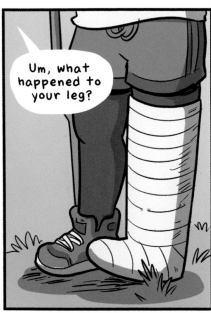

Um, what happened to your leg?

. . .

You're weird.

I know.

It's okay. Not, like, creepy-weird.

Just . . . you'd definitely stick out in my school.

You talked to a bush and made it grow blackberries, and that's . . .

well, weird!

But I promise I won't tell anyone.

Not my dads, or anyone at my school, or anyone at your definitely-not-made-up school.

Thanks.

Well, I've gotta go. Bye, berry boy.

Three years and two months.

pat pat

Are you helping Mom?

We're trying to scry for Sedge, me and some of the younger girls.

Scry?

Use magic to look for him.

But none of the normal bowls we use are working, so I'm looking for something else . . .

You look in a bowl?

In water. In a silver bowl, usually. Silver for the moon.

And you reflect the moon in it, and you stir it counter-clockwise, and --

HOP

He stepped outside the barrier.

That's correct, Tupelo.

We are protected here, because this is a place to be safe and learn.

But outside the standing stones, demons and broken spirits and the fallen roam, preying on humans -- although most people don't know their true nature.

You can't live in this house forever. You must remember that, though they are rare, there are creatures that want to kill you and worse.

That's why it's important to learn to *fight*, and that's why we speak to animal spirits.

You must be strong, because your job will be to protect the humans and the witches from these monsters.

Can't the witches protect themselves?

Sure, with the standing stones and other magics. But witchery takes time, and is better used for other things.

When it comes to battle, to the struggle of life or death . . . that's where we come in.

So tell me . . . did some of you meet animal spirits last night?

Yes, Aquila?

An old badger came to me, and he wanted to wrestle, so I --

-- was a bird, definitely something with feathers, and it told me --

-- so once I caught it, he told me secrets of the treetops and said I would learn his form!

splish

splash

I was sort of looking for you.

Oh, yeah?

BANG

Come on!

Are you supposed to play that sitting down?

Uh, no, genius. Why don't you try?

whoosh

Wow, never mind!

TMP

Why were you looking for me?

I just . . .

I can't talk to anyone in my house!

I want to . . . help and stuff . . . but everyone thinks I'm a freak.

I'm good at . . . this one thing, but it's a thing that only girls do.

But I'm not good at boy stuff, and I just . . .

want to help.

Ugh, tell me about it.

This year at school they stop having co-ed teams, and the guys have *way* more sports than the girls.

They split stuff up for boys and girls at your school?

Not everything. But sports, yeah, and that's what I really like.

At least I have softball, but . . .

I probably won't get to play this year anyway.

BMP

There *is* a moon, so maybe this'll work.

I overheard Mom saying it's more about intent than specifics . . .

Okay, I'll try to show you my mom. I think you'd like her.

Mom. Holly.

How're you doing that?

And that's your house?

It's so funky!

Whoa. Is that a . . .

Hey!

Is that . . . magic?

nod

And you're not supposed to do it?

It's a girl thing.

But . . . I really like it. It's not like I can just . . . not do it.

What else can you do?

I don't know a lot of spells. They're secret.

But I can . . .

Well, you saw, I can make fruit grow.

I can scry, and I can light candles, but it doesn't always work.

I can make a little circle of silence -- I use that one a lot to read.

And I can fix broken things.

Like bones?

No, I meant like . . . broken bowls and things . . .

Could I --

could I pay you or give you something or --

If you could heal my leg . . .

Aster, the doctor said it was a really bad break, and it'll take forever to heal and it still might not be quite right --

Have you seen Aster?

74

I can't fix your leg now.

I might just make it worse, anyway.

But I'll find out how, and I'll come back really soon, I promise.

Okay.

Hey, Aster? Your magic?

I think it's brilliant.

Something that sneaks through our boundaries and evades us at every turn.
It may be an animal spirit, but what would its motivation be?
It may be a demon we've never encountered before.
We need to stay on our guard.
We need to find out how this monster is getting to us, and where it's keeping our boys.
I refuse to believe they're . . . not alive.
If you kids see anything strange --
anything at all --
let us know.

You all have heard tales, my daughters, of the witches of old, who went into battle against rival clans and evil spirits.

We are lucky to live in this time and this country, where there is peace between witches and the evil spirits are not as bold as they once were.

But I cannot promise you lives free of battle -- especially with the evil that seems to have descended on our family.

And so you must learn about our house's weapons, passed down from mother to daughter since time immemorial.

We have four weapons.

They channel and magnify your will, and can perform various tasks depending on what you desire.

The six stones, for example --

toss them and they will tell you things about the future.

They are vessels for your focus. Now, the dagger hilt --

stones - future

Excuse me, Iris?

Yes?

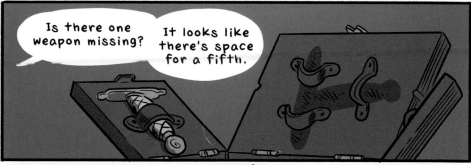

Is there one weapon missing?

It looks like there's space for a fifth.

The sword was stolen before you were born, child, by the traitor Mikasi.

He hoped to use it to give himself unnatural powers, but because he was a *man*, it could only have hurt him or else not worked at all.

The dagger, though lesser than the sword, has unique properties . . .

Is that . . . ?

. . . spying again, that's so weird.

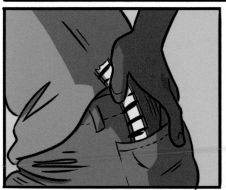

Uh, what?

Where even were you last night?

When Aquila and 'Pelo went missing?

Because your mom was looking for you for ages.

I was on a walk, I said --

Oh, yeah? Alone or with them?

Because when Sedge was taken, you were *right* there.

Yeah! You were the only one to see him get taken.

What are you saying?

We're just saying you're *weird.*

You don't pay attention in class -- when you even come -- and you're always . . . sneaking around.

I didn't -- I don't *sneak!*

Have you ever shifted? I've never seen it, and you're older than Brome!

heh heh

Leave me alone, Linden.

That mean you finally figured it out?

Come on, Aster, show us.

Turn into something *fierce*.

Like this!

Come on, Aster. Did you do something to Sedge and 'Pelo and Aquila?

Just leave me alone, guys --

What's that?

grrrr

THWAK

-- BACK!

What was that?

He did witchery!

Still, Aster?

This magic isn't for you.

I wouldn't even be drawing it with you here if everyone else wasn't in such a tizzy. All these terrible things happening.

SEDGE

Now get --

go back to the house and ask Uncle Kieran if you can help him.

CLK

SLAM

. . . All we know is that something *corrupted* Sedge.

He's still *him*, as far as I can see. The use of his name was efficacious, and . . .

I'll have to look at him with my eyestone in the morning --

But he's been twisted into the worst, most vicious shape he could become.

Think, Iris . . . kidnappers?

Child thieves?

But it *worked!* I thought you might understand . . .

Bad things happen to boys who dabble with witchery.
Yes, and vice versa, too! I've seen it. Ask Grandmother about her brother, Mikasi, sometime ––

I know, but can't I help –– ?

No.

SLAM

And I'm the only one, little shifter
who can teach you how to use it.

Mom?
Can I --

Not now,
Aster!

What do you remember, sweetness?

It's all hazy, like . . . that time I had the really bad fever.

All twisty.

A cave? Did you find me in a cave?

No, but --

flinch

If I could come home afterward, and if I could finally do the magic everyone wants me to do . . .

I don't think my mom and dad would care that I learned from a monster.

But you said you'd heal my leg.

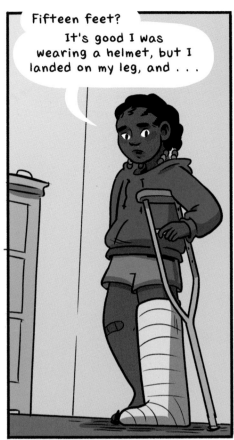

Fifteen feet?

It's good I was wearing a helmet, but I landed on my leg, and . . .

That's . . . terrible. And why . . . ?

I mean, so, you tried to do something you weren't supposed to and you got really hurt?

What are you saying?

The thing is?

I only dared those boys to jump the cliff because I wanted to do it, too.

It was the coolest thing I've ever done, even if I did get hurt. And I'd do it again.

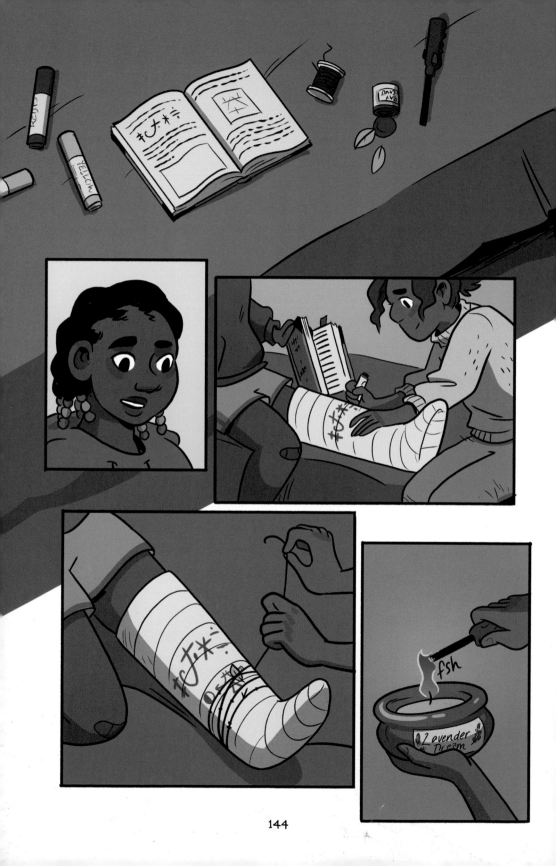

How long's it going to glow, though?

Oh, uh . . . a while. Until "the magic has run its course."

Says to stay off the leg until then, too.

Aster! What are my dads gonna think?

I don't know, but I have to go.

Can't stay out after sunset anymore.

Aw, they wanted you to stay for dinner. We're making meatloaf!

Sorry.

Um, I hope your leg heals okay!

Can I come over later? If it is?

I have an idea.

Uh . . . yeah, but you can't let anyone see you.

If you go down your street and follow that old dirt road about half a mile, you should be able to see the lights from my house off to the left.

Someone might be patrolling, so be sneaky.

And you're not going to call that evil monster thing, right?

You really shouldn't be here, I'll get in so much trouble if --

Aster! Look at my leg!

I ran all the way here!

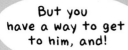

But you have a way to get to him, and! You have the element of surprise! Because you can do *witchery*.

I don't know any spells powerful enough to hurt him.

Weren't you telling me about those weapons? Let's figure out how to get one of them.

Surprise, yeah? I'll stay here, and if something goes wrong, I'll tell your family everything.

There's no magic on *me*.

And then what do I do?

Go rescue your cousins, obviously!

The sword was stolen before you were born, child, by the traitor Mikasi.

TSS SSS

Please work, please work, just take us home --

SCROWWW

CLNK

I've been trying to tell you for a long time.

I love you no matter what, Aster.

We'll figure this out as a family.

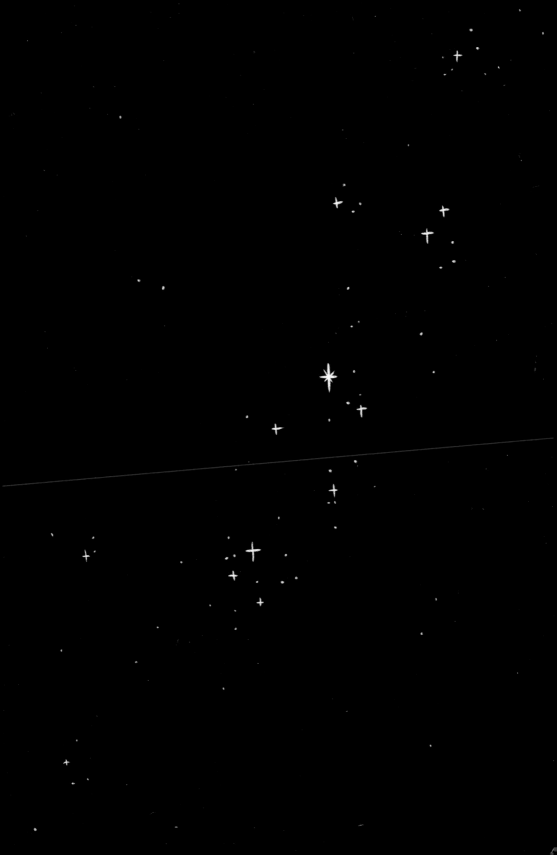

Mom and Dad don't really get it, but . . . I don't know, they haven't kicked me out or anything.

So it all worked out!

Yeah, I guess it did.

What about what's his name -- Mikasi?

He's still in the spell.

I think they don't know what to do with him.

Seeing him . . .

He was like me. I could have been like that.

But I won't be.

You? You're way too nice.

Maybe.

If you're studying to be a witch and everything, you'll be really busy, won't you?

You probably won't be able to come over here anymore.

ACKNOWLEDGMENTS

I've drawn several graphic novels, but this is the first one I've written, and it's close to my heart.

I'd like to thank my mom, dad, and everyone else in our family for being so supportive of my unusual interests and implausible goals. I feel your love every day and I hope you feel mine, too.

I'd like to thank my friends — the people I know from summer camp, art school, comic conventions, animation, and the Internet. Your talent pushes me to work harder, and your kindness makes me a better person.

I'd like to thank my agent, Jen Linnan, who is fiercely smart, warm, and has been with me for every step on this journey.

I'd also like to thank my editor, Amanda Maciel, and my art director, Phil Falco, whose expertise and advice were a huge help in bringing this book into the world.

I drew this book during a year of many changes, and my partner was with me through them all. She believed in me even when I didn't. Thank you, Noelle — I love you and the home we've made together so very much.

DEVELOPMENT
ART

Aster, along with all the other kids in the family, mostly wears hand-me-downs, and accessorizes with protection charms made for him by his mother. His favorite color is purple and he doesn't like getting haircuts.

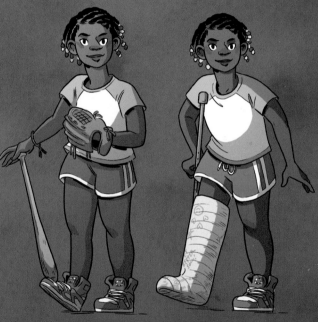

Even when Charlie has her leg in a cast, she still dresses like she's ready to play basketball or baseball at the drop of a hat. In an earlier draft of this story, she didn't have a broken leg, which is why there's a design of her without a cast.

This is early concept art of Aster, when I thought he'd be older. I always knew, though, that he liked to find out-of-the-way places to read through his spell book.

Holly is a perfect witch. She's powerful, practical, beautiful, and kind, and I wanted her character design to reflect that.

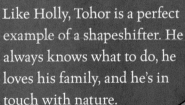

Like Holly, Tohor is a perfect example of a shapeshifter. He always knows what to do, he loves his family, and he's in touch with nature.

I had a lot of different designs for Mikasi, but I decided in the end to make him into a kind of dragon monster. He used magic to force himself to transform so many times that he became a mishmash of different animals—a coyote's face, a crocodile's body, and a human's hands.

MOLLY KNOX OSTERTAG

grew up in the forests of upstate New York, where she spent the first half of her childhood reading about fantastical adventures and the second half acting them out with foam swords at a live-action role-playing group. She graduated in 2014 from the School of Visual Arts, where she studied cartooning and illustration; she now lives in Los Angeles, California. *The Witch Boy* is her middle-grade graphic novel debut. You can visit Molly online at www.mollyostertag.com.